GERALD'S NEW

By Nicola Carroll

Illustrated by **meri_rehman**

Gerald the spider lives upstairs.
Spinning his webs, he has no cares.

Watching the Smyths go in and out.
There is one thing Gerald is curious about.

Putting shoes on their feet? He doesn't know why.

But thinks he would like to give it a try.

He jumps on a bus. He knows where to stop.

Just outside a large shoe shop.

Gerald looks at the shelves.
Not knowing what to choose,

he needs some help to find his new shoes.

"How may I help?" The assistant is very polite.

"I'd like a new pair of shoes",
Gerald squeals with delight.

"A pair of shoes. That's only two!"

"Please take a seat and I'll ask you to wait."

"I'll go to the store and try to find eight!"

"How about these? They are lovely and shiny."

"I'm afraid they don't fit. My feet are too tiny!"

"Try some boots" the assistant says with a grin.

"I'm not too keen. They come up to my chin!"

"Some running shoes. Let's give these a shot."

"Good grief" cries Gerald. "I'm stuck in a knot!"

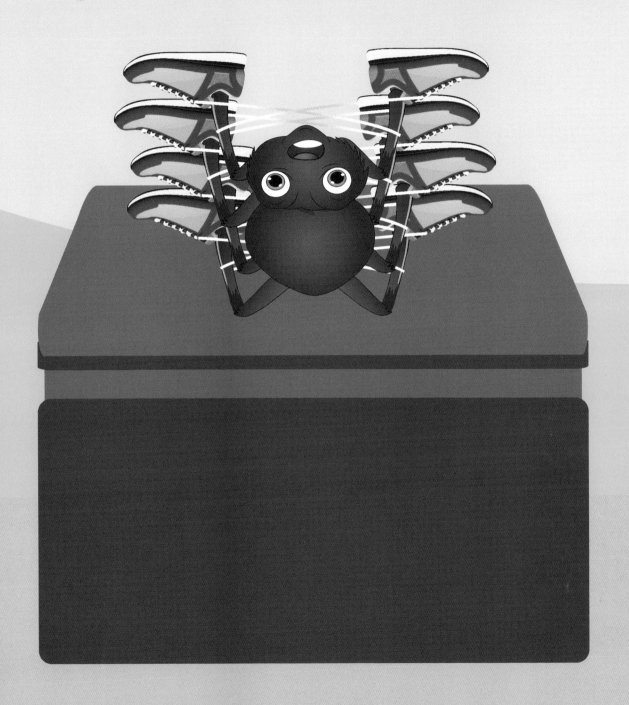

"I have found them", says the assistant, looking very cheery.

"Oh I hope so", says Gerald.
He is now very weary.

Gerald puts them on,
and as he walks on the ground,

they make the most wonderful, wonderful, tackety sound.

tack

tack

tack

tack

tack

tack

tack

tack

"These are perfect!"
yells Gerald without any doubt.

I can't wait to wear them out and about.

Now back at the Smyths, whether at work, rest or play,

Gerald wears his new shoes all night and all day.

But what's that strange noise?"
The Smyths try to guess.

They haven't a clue, they have to confess.

Is it mice? bats? birds? to name but a few.

No...

It's Gerald's tackety shoes!

tack

tack

tack

tack

tack

tack

tack

tack

If only they knew!

© 2020 by **Nicola Carroll**

Printed in Poland
by Amazon Fulfillment
Poland Sp. z o.o., Wrocław

64669663R00023